This igloo book belongs to:

....

igloobooks

Published in 2014
by Igloo Books Ltd
Cottage Farm
Sywell
NN6 0BJ
www.igloobooks.com

LEO002 0514
2 4 6 8 10 9 7 5 3 1
ISBN 978-1-78440-075-0

Illustrated by Lee Robinson

Printed and manufactured in China

There's a
Monster
Under
My
Bed!

Lee Robinson

igloobooks

"I think there's something under the bed," thought Billy. In fact, he was sure he heard a hungry belly...

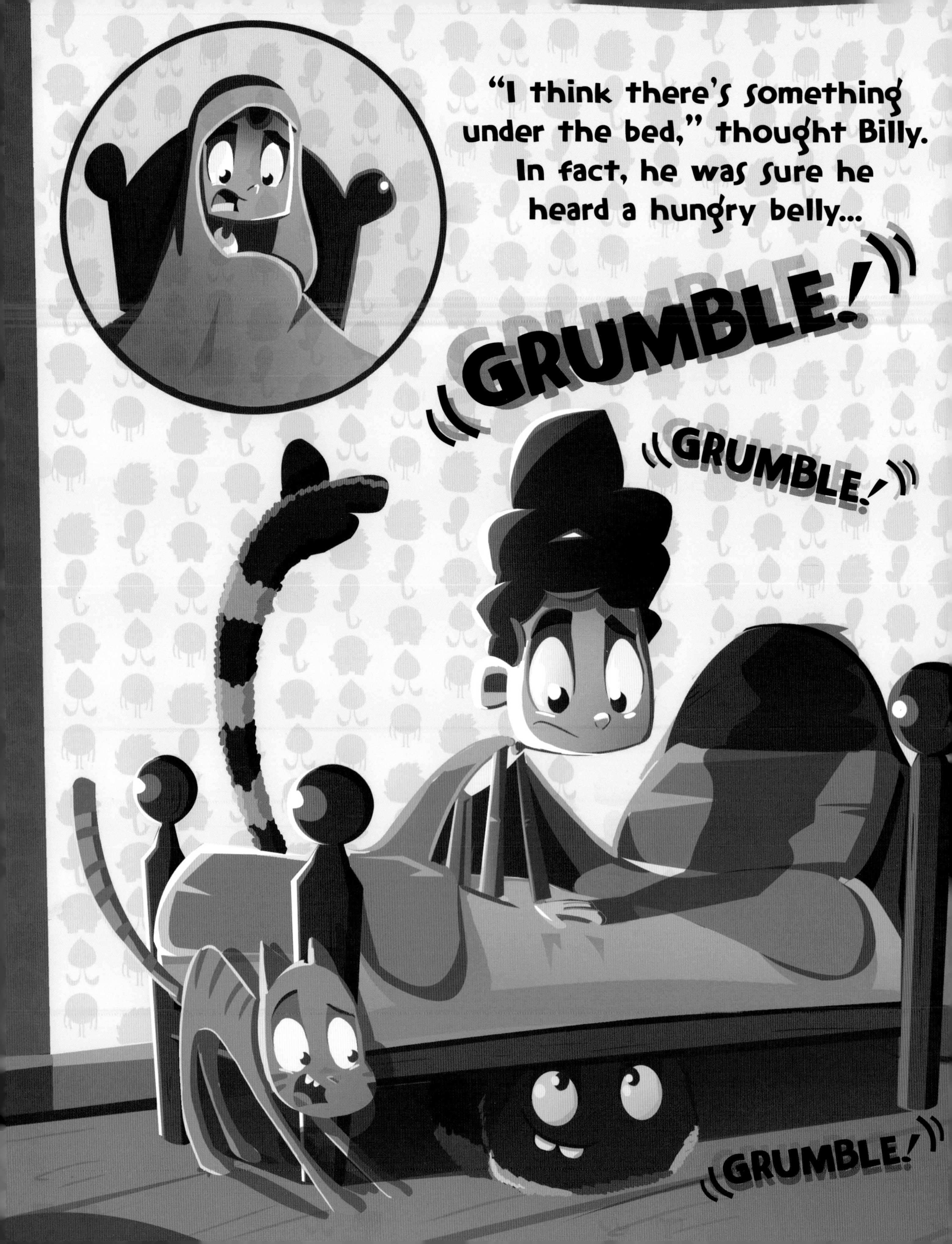

Billy pulled his duvet tightly over his head, **but** the grumbling got even louder. Eventually, he decided to take a look.

Very slowly, he peered **DOWN** underneath the bed...

HHHHHH!

It's a
monster!

As quick as a flash, Billy raced out of his bedroom, down the stairs and hid in a cupboard.

SSSSHHHHHHHHHH!

A big, red, friendly face stared at him in surprise.

"Eat you?"

said the monster, sticking out his long, slimy tongue.

BLEAR

"I'm sure you'd taste horrible! Do you have something nicer to eat? I'm starving!"

HHHHHH!

"There are some cookies in the cookie jar," replied Billy. "I suppose you can have one."

As Billy carefully opened the jar of tasty cookies, the naughty monster found the fridge full of fresh food behind him.

"Ooh, what delicious, tasty treats!" cried the monster, as he stuffed his face with cream buns and caramel cheesecake.

MUNCH! GOBBLE! SLURP!

Food and drink flew all over the room as the monster feasted!

"What's going on in here?"

said Billy's mum, standing in the doorway.

Billy spun around, still holding the cookie jar. Sloppy food dripped down the cupboards and walls.

The monster was nowhere to be seen.

"It wasn't me, Mum," said Billy.
"It was a monster!"

"I see," said Mum, rolling her eyes.
"Well, perhaps you should take him
upstairs while I sort out this mess."

In the living room,
the monster was
jumping on the sofa.
"That was a great feast,"
he said, with a
huge grin.
"Now let's have
some fun!"

The monster

leaPt

off the sofa and
bounced all around
the room...

BOING! BOING!

... sending a neat pile of freshly
cleaned clothes flying through the
air and onto the floor.

"Oh, no!" cried Billy, as the living room door **swung** open suddenly. Billy's mum stared around the room, looking quite shocked.

"What a mess!" said Billy's mum.

The monster had disappeared again.
"I want this room tidied up
before breakfast."
She rolled her eyes again and
closed the door behind her.

Billy was fed up.
"You keep getting me in trouble,"

he said crossly, as the monster crawled out from his hiding place.

The monster looked around the room at all of the mess.

"Sorry, Billy," said the monster, feeling a little embarrassed.

"I just wanted to have some fun.

What can I do to make it better?"

"Why don't you help me tidy this room?" asked Billy. "It's in quite a mess!"

WHOOOOOSHH!

"It'll be done in no time," said the monster, whizzing around the room at top speed.

Billy watched, amazed, as the monster **twirled** and **SPUN,** flinging toys and clothes back into their places once more.

"It's quite handy having a monster around, after all," thought Billy to himself.

When the room was tidy again,
Billy sat down for breakfast.

"Don't forget
a plate for
the monster,"

he said.
Mum winked and
dished up an
extra helping...
just in case!